Dear Parent:
Your child's love of rea

10666828

Every child learns to read in a different way and at his or her own speed. You can help your young reader improve and become more confident by encouraging his or her own interests and abilities. You can also guide your child's spiritual development by reading stories with biblical values and Bible stories, like I Can Read! books published by Zonderkidz. From books your child reads with you to the first books he or she reads alone, there are I Can Read! books for every stage of reading:

SHARED READING
Basic language, word repetition, and whimsical illustrations, ideal for sharing with your emergent reader.

BEGINNING READING
Short sentences, familiar words, and simple concepts for children eager to read on their own.

READING WITH HELP
Engaging stories, longer sentences, and language play for developing readers.

READING ALONE
Complex plots, challenging vocabulary, and high-interest topics for the independent reader.

ADVANCED READING
Short paragraphs, chapters, and exciting themes for the perfect bridge to chapter books.

I Can Read! books have introduced children to the joy of reading since 1957. Featuring award-winning authors and illustrators and a fabulous cast of beloved characters, I Can Read! books set the standard for beginning readers.

A lifetime of discovery begins with the magical words **"I Can Read!"**

Visit www.icanread.com for information on enriching your child's reading experience.
Visit www.zonderkidz.com for more Zonderkidz I Can Read! titles.

Don't hold back good from
those who are worthy of it.
Don't hold it back when you can help.

—Proverbs 3:27

www.zonderkidz.com

Jake Helps Out
Copyright © 2007 by Crystal Bowman
Illustrations © 2007 by Karen Maizel
Originally published in *Jonathan James Says, "I Can Help"* © 1995
ISBN-10: 0-310-71457-5
ISBN-13: 978-0-310-71457-6

Requests for information should be addressed to:
Grand Rapids, Michigan 49530

Library of Congress Cataloging-in-Publication Data

Bowman, Crystal.
Jake helps out / story by Crystal Bowman ; pictures by Karen Maizel.
p. cm. – (Jake Biblical values series) (I can read! level 2)
Summary: Jake wants very much to help his family get ready for
a picnic at the lake, but everything he does seems to turn out wrong.
ISBN-13: 978-0-310-71457-6 (softcover)
ISBN-10: 0-310-71457-5 (softcover)
[1. Helpfulness–Fiction. 2. Family life–Fiction. 3. Christian life
–Fiction.] I. Maizel, Karen, ill. II. Title.
PZ7.B68335Jai 2007
[E]–dc22
2006029331

All Scripture quotations unless otherwise noted are taken from the *Holy Bible: New International Reader's Version*®. NIrV®. Copyright © 1995, 1996, 1998 by International Bible Society. Used by permission of Zondervan. All rights reserved.

All rights reserved. No part of this publication may be reproduced, stored in a retrieval system, or transmitted in any form or by any means—electronic, mechanical, photocopy, recording, or any other—except for brief quotations in printed reviews, without the prior permission of the publisher.

Zonderkidz is a trademark of Zondervan.

Art Direction: Laura Maitner-Mason
Cover and Interior Design: Jody Langley

Printed in China

07 08 09 10 11 • 10 9 8 7 6 5 4 3 2 1

Jake Helps Out

story by Crystal Bowman

pictures by Karen Maizel

“When are we going to the lake?”

asked Jake.

“After breakfast, Jake,” said Mother.

“After I wash the dishes

and pack the picnic basket,”

said Father.

Jake ate a bowl of cereal.

"I want some cereal too,"

said his little sister, Kelly.

Jake put cereal in Kelly's bowl

and poured the milk.

Splash! It went all over the table.

“I’m sorry,” said Jake.

“I just wanted to help.”

Father rinsed his soapy hands.

“I will wipe it up,” he said.

Jake saw the dirty dishes
soaking in the kitchen sink.
He reached into the soapy water
to wash a big round plate.
The plate slipped out of his hands.

Crash! It broke into tiny pieces

all over the floor.

“I’m sorry,” said Jake.

“I just wanted to help.”

Mother set down the picnic basket.

“I will get the broom,” she said.

Jake saw the picnic basket

on the counter.

He put in a box of cheese crackers.

He put in a bag of chocolate cookies.

He put in a big jar of pickles.

Oops! The lid came off the jar.

CHEESE
CRACKERS

Pee-yew! Sticky, stinky pickle juice spilled all over the picnic basket.

"I'm sorry," said Jake.

"I just wanted to help."

"We don't need your help right now,"

Mother said.

Jake went to his bedroom.

"Nobody needs my help," he thought.

Kelly came to his door.

"Do you want to play?" she asked.

"I want to help," said Jake,

"but I just get in the way."

Kelly took a book from the shelf.

“Read me a story, Jake,” she said.

Jake read the book to Kelly.

“Read me another one,” said Kelly.

They read another book,

and then they read another book.

Knock! knock! knock!

“Who’s there?” Jake asked.

"It's me," said Mother.

"It's time to go to the lake!"

"Yippee!" said Jake and Kelly.

It was sunny and warm at the lake.

Jake and Kelly played in the sand.

“I’ll show you

how to make a sandcastle,”

Jake told Kelly.

They built a big golden castle
with three tall towers.

Then they splashed in the water.

"I will teach you how to swim,"

said Jake.

He even showed Kelly how to float.

Jake and Kelly sat on their towels
in the warm sun.
Father opened the picnic basket.
Jake ate three cheese crackers
and one chocolate cookie.
He bit into a big, juicy pickle.

COOKIES

"You were a big helper today,"

Mother told Jake.

"No, I wasn't," said Jake.

"I poured milk all over the table.

I broke a plate on the floor.

And I spilled sticky, stinky

pickle juice in the picnic basket."

“Those were just little accidents,”

Father said.

“Everyone has them now and then.”

“You were a big helper
when you read to Kelly,” said Mother.
“That’s right,” said Father.
“You helped her make a sandcastle,
and you taught her how to swim.”

"You are important to our family,"

said Mother.

"I am?" asked Jake.

"Yes, Jake," said Father.

"God made you a big helper.

Our family needs a big helper."

Jake finished eating his pickle.

He was happy that God made him

to be a big helper.

He was happy his family needed him.

And he was happy being Jake.